# How the Rabbit Caught the Tiger

A Korean Folk Tale

retold by Anne O'Brien
illustrated by Jean and Mou-sien Tseng

Open Court Publishing Company

Printed in the United States of America

ISBN 0-8126-1288-4

10 9

One winter's eve,
a mighty and hungry tiger
caught a tiny rabbit.

"Do not eat me!" cried the rabbit.
"I am too small to make a good meal.
If you let me go, I will show you
how to catch all the fish you can eat!"

The greedy tiger waited longer.
It grew colder and colder.
His tail grew heavier.

Finally the sun came up.
The tiger's tail was very heavy.
"It is time!" called the tiger.
"I am pulling the fish out now!"

The tiger pulled and pulled,
but his tail did not come out of the river.
It was frozen in the ice!
"I'm going to get you, rabbit!"
roared the angry tiger.
But he could not budge at all.

The rabbit giggled and scampered away.
He had tricked the mighty tiger!